Edward Bulwer Lytton, Frank O. Small

The Secret Way

A Lost Tale of Miletus

Edward Bulwer Lytton, Frank O. Small

The Secret Way
A Lost Tale of Miletus

ISBN/EAN: 9783337343439

Printed in Europe, USA, Canada, Australia, Japan

Cover: Foto ©Andreas Hilbeck / pixelio.de

More available books at **www.hansebooks.com**

THE SECRET WAY

A LOST TALE OF MILETUS

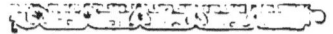

BY

EDWARD BULWER LYTTON

ILLUSTRATED BY F. O. SMALL

BOSTON
D. LOTHROP COMPANY
WASHINGTON STREET OPPOSITE BROMFIELD

LIST OF ILLUSTRATIONS.

ARGUMENT.

THE very striking legend which suggests the following poem is found in Athenæus, Book XIII. CHAP. XXXV. It is there given as a quotation from the "History of Alexander, by Chares of Mitylene." The author adds, that "the story is often told by the barbarians who dwell in Asia, and is exceedingly admired; and they have painted representations of the story in their temples and palaces, and also in their private houses." In constructing the plot of the poem, I have made some variations in incident and *dénouement* from the meager outlines of the old romance preserved in Athenæus, with a view of heightening the interest which springs from the groundwork of the legend. I should add that the name of the Scythian king's daughter is changed from Odatis — which, for narrative purpose, a little too nearly resembles that of her father, Omartes — to Argiope: a name more Hellenic, it is true, but it may be reasonably doubted whether that of Odatis be more genuinely Scythian. For the sake of euphony, the name of the Persian Prince is softened from Zariadres to Zariades. This personage is said by the author whom Athenæus quotes to have been the brother of Hystaspes, and to have held dominion over the country from above the Caspian Gates to the river Tanais (the modern Don). Although the hero of the legend would have been, as described, of purely Persian origin (a royal Achæmenian), and the people subjected to him would not have belonged to Media proper, in the poem he is sometimes called the Mede and his people Medes, according to a usage sufficiently common among Greek writers when speaking generally of the rulers and people of the great Persian Empire. It may scarcely be worth while to observe that though in subsequent tales where the Hellenic deities are more or less prominently introduced or referred to, their Hellenic names are assigned to them, yet in the passing allusions made in this poem to the God of War or the Goddess of Morning. it was judged more agreeable to the general reader to designate those deities by the familiar names of Mars and Aurora rather than by the Greek appellations of Ares and Eos.   EDWARD BULWER LYTTON.

THE SECRET WAY

A LOST TALE OF MILETUS

THE SECRET WAY

OMARTES, King of the wide plains which,
  north
Of Tanais, pasture steeds for Scythian Mars,
Forsook the simple ways
  And Nomad tents of his unconquered fathers;

And in the fashion of the neighboring Medes,
Built a great city girt with moat and wall,
  And in the midst thereof
    A regal palace dwarfing piles in Susa,

With vast foundations rooted into earth,
And crested summits soaring into Heaven,
   And gates of triple brass,
       Siege-proof as portals welded by the Cyclops.

One day Omartes, in his pride of heart,
Led his High Priest, Teleutias, thro' his halls,
   And chilled by frigid looks.
       When counting on warm praise, asked " What
           is wanting ?

" Where is beheld the palace of a king,
So stored with all that doth a king beseem ;
   The woofs of Phrygian   looms.
       The gold of Colchis,   and   the   pearls of
                                                  Ormus,

" Couches of ivory sent from farthest Ind,
Sidonian crystal, and Corinthian bronze,
   Egypt's vast symbol gods,
     And those imagined into men by Hellas ;

" Stored not in tents that tremble to a gale,
But chambers firm-based as the Pyramids,
   And breaking into spray
     The surge of Time, as Gades breaks the ocean ? "

" Nor thou nor I the worth of these things now
Can judge ; we stand too near them," said the sage.
   None till they reach the tomb
     Scan with just eye the treasures of the palace.

" But for thy building — as we speak, I feel
Thro' all the crannies pierce an icy wind
   More bitter than the blasts
     Which howled without the tents of thy rude
       fathers.

" Thou hast forgot to bid thy masons close
The chinks of stone against Calamity."
 The sage inclined his brow,
  Shivered, and, parting, round him wrapt his
   mantle.

The King turned, thoughtful, to a favorite chief,
The rudest champion of the polished change
 That fixed the wain-borne homes
  Of the wild Scythian, and encamped a city;

" Heard'st thou the Sage, brave Seuthes ? " asked
  the King.
" Yea, the priest deemed thy treasures insecure,
 And fain would see them safe
  In his own temple." The King smiled on
   Seuthes.

Unto this Scythian monarch's nuptial bed
But one fair girl, Argiope, was born :
 For whom no earthly throne
  Soared from the level of his fond ambition.

SHIVERED, AND, PARTING, ROUND HIM WRAPT HIS MANTLE

To her, indeed, had Aphroditè given
Beauty, that royalty which subjects kings,
   Sweet with unconscious charm,
     And modest as the youngest of the Graces.

Men blest her when she moved before their eyes
Shamefaced, as blushing to be born so fair,
   Mild as that child of gods
     Violet-crowned Athens hallowing named
       " Pity." *

Now, of a sudden, over that bright face
There fell the shadow of some troubled thought,
   As cloud, from purest dews
     Updrawn, makes sorrowful a star in heaven :

And as a nightingale that having heard
A perfect music from some master's lyre,
   Steals into coverts lone,
     With her own melodies no more contented,

But haunted by the strain, till then unknown,
Seeks to re-sing it back, herself to charm,
   Seeks still and ever fails,
      Missing the key-note which unlocks the music;

So, from her former pastimes in the choir
Of comrade virgins, stole Argiope,
   Lone amid summer leaves
      Brooding that thought, which was her joy and
         trouble.

The king discerned the change in his fair child,
And questioned oft, yet could not learn the cause;
   The sunny bridge between
      The lip and heart which childhood builds was
         broken.

Not more Aurora, stealing into heaven,
Conceals the mystic treasures of the deep
   Whence with chaste blush she comes,
      Than virgin bosoms guard their earliest secret.

Omartes sought the priest, to whose wise heart
So dear the maiden, he was wont to say
    That grains of crackling salt
        From her pure hand, upon the altar sprinkled,

Sent up a flame to loftier heights in heaven
Than that which rolled from hecatombs in smoke.
    " King," said the musing seer,
        " Behold, the woodbine, opening infant blossoms,

" Perfumes the bank whose herbage hems it round,
From its own birthplace drinking in delight ;
    Later, its instinct stirs ;
        Fain would it climb — to climb forbidden,
            creepeth,

" Its lot obeys its yearning to entwine ;
Around the oak it weaves a world of flowers ;
   Or, listless drooping, trails
      Dejected tendrils lost mid weed and brier.

" There needs no construing to my parable :
As is the woodbine's, so the woman's life :
   Look round the forest kings,
      And to the stateliest wed thy royal blossom."

Sharp is a father's pang when comes the hour
In which his love contents his child no more,
   And the sweet wonted smile
      Fades from his hearthstone to rejoice a
      stranger's.

But soon from parent love dies thought of self ;
Omartes, looking round the Lords of earth,
   In young Zariades
      Singled the worthiest of his peerless daughter ;

Scion of that illustrious hero-stem,
Which in great Cyrus bore the loftiest flower
  Purpled by Orient suns ;
    Stretched his vast satrapies, engulfing king-
      doms,

From tranquil palmgroves fringing Caspian waves,
To the bleak marge of stormy Tanais ;
  On Scythia bordering thus,
    No foe so dread, and no ally so potent.

Perilous boundary-rights by Media claimed
O'er that great stream which, laving Scythian plains,
  Europe from Asia guards,
    The Persian Prince, in wedding Scythia's
      daughter,

Might well resign, in pledge of lasting peace.
But ill the project of Omartes pleased
  His warlike free-born chiefs,
    And ill the wilder tribes of his fierce people ;

For Scyth and Mede had long been as those winds
Whose very meeting in itself is storm,
   Yet the King's will prevailed,
     Confirmed, when wavering, by his trusted
       Scuthes.

He, the fierce leader of the fiercest horde,
Won from the wild by greed of gain and power,
   Stood on the bound between
     Man social and man savage, dark and massive :

So rugged was he that men deemed him true,
So secret was he that men deemed him wise,
   And he had grown so great,
     The throne was lost behind the subject's
       shadow.

In the advice he whispered to the king
He laid the key-stone of ambitious hope,
   This marriage with the Mede
     Would leave to heirs remote the Scythian
       kingdom,

Sow in men's minds vague fears of foreign rule,
Which might, if cultured, spring to armed revolt.
  In armed revolt how oft
    Kings disappear, and none dare call it murder.

And when a crown falls bloodstained in the dust,
The strong man standing nearest to its fall
  Takes it and crowns himself;
    And heirs remote are swept from earth as rebels.

Of peace and marriage-rites thus dreamed the king;
Of graves and thrones the traitor : while the fume
  From altars, loud with prayer
    To speed the Scythian envoys, darkened heaven.

A hardy prince was young Zariades,
Scorning the luxuries of the loose-robed Mede,
  Cast in the antique mould
    Of men whose teaching thewed the soul of
      Cyrus.

" To ride, to draw the bow, to speak the truth,
Sufficed to Cyrus," said the prince, when child.
    " Astyages knew more,"
        Answered the Magi — " Yes, and lost his king-
            doms."

Yet there was in this prince the eager mind
Which needs must think, and therefore needs must
        learn ;
    Natures, whose roots strike deep,
        Clear their own way, and win to light in grow-
            ing.

His that rare beauty which both charms and awes
The popular eye ; his the life-gladdening smile ;
    His the death-dooming frown :
        That which he would he could ; — men loved
            and feared him.

Now of a sudden over this grand brow
There fell the gloom of some unquiet thought,
    As when the south wind sweeps
        Sunshine from Hadria in a noon of summer :

And as a stag, supreme among the herd,
With lifted crest inhaling lusty air,
  Smit by a shaft from far,
    Deserts his lordly range amidst the pasture,

And thro' dim woodlands with drooped antlers creeps
To the cool marge of rush-grown watersprings;
  So from all former sports,
    Contest, or converse with once-loved companions,

Stole the young prince through unfrequented groves,
To gaze with listless eyes on lonely streams.
  All, wondering, marked the change,
    None dared to question: he had no fond father.

Now, in the thick of this his altered mood,
Arrived the envoys of the Scythian king,
  Reluctant audience found,
    And spoke to ears displeased their sovereign's
      message.

" Omartes greets Zariades the Mede
Between the realms of both there rolls a river
   Inviolate to the Scyth,
      Free to no keels but those the Scythian char-
        ters :

" Yet have thy subjects outraged oft its waves,
And pirate foray on our northern banks
   Ravaged the flocks and herds,
      Till Scythian riders ask 'Why sleeps the
        Ruler?'

" Still, loth to fan the sparks which leap to flame
Reddening the nations, from the breath of kings;
   We have not sought thy throne
      With tales of injury or appeals to justice;

" But searching in our inmost heart to find
The gentlest bond wherewith to link our realms,
   Make Scyth and Mede akin,
      By household ties their royal chiefs uniting,

" We strip our crown of its most precious gem,
Proffering to thee our child Argiope:
  So let the Median Queen
    Be the mild guardian of the Scythian river."

Lifting his brow, replied Zariades:
" Great rivers are the highways of the world :
  The Tanais laves my shores ;
    For those who dwell upon my shores I claim it.

" If pirates land on either side for prey,
My banks grow herdsmen who can guard their herds ;
  Take, in these words, reply
    To all complaints that threaten
      Median subjects.

" But for the gentler phrase wherewith your king
Stoops to a proffer, yet implies command,
    I pray you, in return,
      To give such thanks as soften most refusal.

" Thanks are a language kings are born to hear,
But speak not glibly till they near their fall.
    To guard his Scythian realm,
      On the Mede's throne the Scyth would place
       his daughter;

" I should deceive him if I said ' Agreed.'
No throne, methinks, hath room for more than one;
    Where a Queen's lips decide
      Or peace or war, she slays the king her hus-
       band.

" Thus thinking, did I wed this Scythian maid.
It were no marriage between Mede and Scyth;
    Nor wrong I unseen charms;
      Love, we are told, comes like the wind from
       heaven

" Not at our bidding, but its own free will.
And so depart — and pardon my plain speech.
   That which I think I say,
     Offending oft-times, but deceiving never."

So he dismissed them, if with churlish words,
With royal presents, and to festal pomps.
   But one, by Median law
     Nearest his throne, the chief priest of the Magi,

Having heard all with not unprescient fears,
Followed the Prince and urged recall of words
   Which, sent from king to king,
     Are fraught with dragon seeds, whose growth
       is armies.

Mute, as if musing in himself, the Prince
Heard the wise counsel to its warning close.
   Then, with a gloomy look,
     Gazed on the reader of the stars, and
       answered —

"Leave thou to me that which to me belongs;
My people need the Tanais for their rafts;
    Or soon or late that need
        Strings the Mede's bow, and mounts the Scyth-
            ian rider.

"Mage, I would pluck my spirit from the hold
Of a strong phantasy, which, night and day,
    Haunts it, unsinews life,
        And makes my heart the foe of my own reason.

"Perchance in war the gods ordain my cure;
And courting war, I to myself give peace."
    Startled by these wild words,
        The Mage, in trust-alluring arts long-practised,

Led on the Prince to unfold their hidden sense;
And having bound the listener by the oath
    Mage never broke, to hold
        Sacred the trust, the King thus told his trouble.

" Know that each night (thro' three revolving moons)
An image comes before me in a dream ;
  Ever the same sweet face,
   Lovely as that which blest the Carian's slum-
    ber.†

" Nought mid the dark-eyed daughters of the East,
Nought I have ever seen in waking hours,
  Rivals in charm this shape
   Which hath no life — unless a dream hath sub-
    stance.

" But never yet so clearly visible,
Nor with such joy in its celestial smile
  Hath come the visitant,
   Making a temple of the soul it hallows,

" As in the last night's vision ; there it stooped
Over my brow, with tresses that I touched,
  With love in bashful eyes,
   With breath whose fragrance lingered yet in
    waking.

" And balmed the morn, as when a dove, that brings
Ambrosia to Olympus, sheds on earth
   Drops from a passing wing:
      Surely the vision made itself thus living

" To test my boast, that truth so fills this soul
It could not lodge a falsehood ev'n in dream:
   Wonderest thou, Magian, now,
      Why I refuse to wed the Scythian's daughter?

" And if I thus confide to thee a tale
I would not whisper into ears profane,
   'Tis that where reason ends,
      Men have no choice between the Gods and
        Chaos.

" Ye Magi are the readers of the stars,
Versed in the language of the world of dreams:
   Wherefore consult thy lore,
      And tell me if Earth hold a mortal maiden

" In whom my nightly vision breathes and moves.
If not, make mine such talismans and spells,
   As banish from the soul
     Dreams that annul its longing for the daylight."

Up to his lofty fire-tower climbed the Mage,
Explored the stars and drew Chaldaean schemes;
   Thrid the dark maze of books
     Opening on voids beyond the bounds of
       Nature;

Placed crystal globes in hands of infants pure;
Invoked the demons haunting impious graves;
   And all, alas, in vain;
     The dream, adjured against itself to witness,

Refused to wander from the gate of horn,
To stars, scrolls, crystals, infants, demons, proof.
   Foiled of diviner lore
     The Mage resumed his wisdom as a mortal;

And since no Mage can own his science fails,
But where that solves not, still solution finds,
   So he resought the King,
      Grave-browed as one whose brain holds Truth
        new-captured :

Saying, " O King, the shape thy dreams have glassed
Is of the Colchian Mother of the Medes ;
   When, on her dragon car,
      From faithless Jason rose sublime Medea,

" Refuge at Athens she with Ægeus found ;
To him espoused she bore one hero-son,
   Medus, the Sire of Medes ;
      And if that form no earthly shape resembles

" What marvel ? for her beauty witched the world,
Ev'n in an age when woman lured the gods ;
   Retaining yet dread powers
      (For memories die not) of her ancient magic,

. . . . IN WRATH AGAINST THE STARS
THE MAGE RESOUGHT HIS TOWER.

" Her spirit lingers in these Orient airs,
And guards the children of her latest love,
   Thus, hovering over thee,
     She warms thy heart to love in her — those
       children.

" As in her presence thou didst feel thy soul
Lodged in a temple, so the Queen commands
   That thou restore the fanes
     And deck the altars where her Medus wor-
       shiped :

" And in the spirit-breath which balmed the morn
Is symbolized the incense on our shrines,
   Which, as thou renderest here,
     Shall waft thee after death to the Immortals.

" Seek, then, no talisman against the dream,
Obey its mandates, and return its love ;
   So shall thy reign be blest,
     And in Zariades revive a Medus."

" Friend,' sighed the King,
   "albeit I   needs
         must own
All dreams mean temples, where
   a Mage explains,
Yet when a young man dreams
   Of decking altars, 'tis not for
      Medea."

He said and turned to lose himself in groves,
Shunning the sun. In wrath against the stars
   The Mage resought his tower.
      And that same day went back the Scythian
         envoys.

But from the night which closed upon that day,
The image of the dream began to fade,
   Fainter and paler seen,
      With saddened face and outlines veiled ї
         vapor ;

At last it vanished as a lingering star
Fades on Cithæron from a Mænad's eyes,
    Mid cymbal, fife and horn,
        When sunrise flashes on the Car of Panthers.

As the dream fled, broke war upon the land:
The Scythian hosts had crossed the Tanais.
    And, where the dreamer dreamed,
        An angry King surveyed his Asian armies.

Who first in fault, the Scythian or the Mede,
Who first broke compact, or transgressed a bound,
    Historic scrolls dispute
        As Scyth or Mede interprets dreams in story.

Enough for war when two brave nations touch,
With rancor simmering in the hearts of kings;
    War is the child of cloud
        Oftentimes stillest just before the thunder.

The armies met in that vast plain whereon
The Chaldee, meting out the earth, became
　　The scholar of the stars, —
　　　　A tombless plain, yet has it buried empires.

At first the Scythian horsemen, right to left,
Broke wings by native Medes outstretched for
　　　　　　flight,
　　But in the central host
　　　　Stood Persia's sons, the mountain race of
　　　　　　Cyrus;

And in their midst, erect in golden car
With looks of scorn, Zariades the King;
　　And at his trumpet voice
　　　　Steed felt as man that now began the battle.

" Up, sons of Persia, Median women fly;
And leave the field to us whom gods made men:
　　The Scythian chases well
　　　　Yon timorous deer; now let him front the
　　　　　　lions."

He spoke, and light-touched by his charioteer
Rushed his white steeds down the quick-parted
       lines;
  The parted lines quick-closed,
    Following that car as after lightning follow

The hail and whirlwind of collected storm:
The Scyths had scattered their own force in chase,
  As torrents split in rills
    The giant waves whose gathered might were
      deluge;

And, as the Scythian strength is in the charge
Of its fierce riders, so that charge, misspent,
  Left weak the ignobler ranks,
    Fighting on foot; alert in raid or skirmish,

And skilled in weapons striking foes from far,
But all untaught to front with levelled spears,
  And rampart line of shields,
    The serried onslaught of converging battle:

Wavering, recoiling, turning oft, they fled ;
Omartes was not with them to uphold ;
   Foremost himself had rode
      Heading the charge by which the Medes were
         scattered ;

And when, believing victory won, he turned
His bloody reins back to the central war,
   Behold, — a cloud of dust,
      And thro' the cloud the ruins of an army !

At sunset, sole king on that plain, reigned Death.
Far off, the dust-cloud rolled ; far off, behind
   A dust-cloud followed fast ;
      The hunted and the hunter, Flight and
         Havoc.

With the scant remnant of his mighty host
(Many who 'scaped the foe forsook their chief
   For plains more safe than walls),
      The Scythian King repassed his brazen
         portals.

SOLE KING ON THAT PLAIN, REIGNED DEATH.

In haste he sent to gather fresh recruits
Among the fiercest tribes his fathers ruled,
  They whom a woman led
    When to her feet they tossed the head of
      Cyrus.

And the tribes answered — " Let the Scythian King
Return repentant to old Scythian ways,
  And laugh with us at foes.
    Wains know no sieges — Freedom moves her
      cities."

Soon came the Victor with his Persian guards,
And all the rallied vengeance of his Medes;
  One night, sprang up dread camps
    With lurid watch-lights circling doomèd ram-
      parts,

As hunters round the wild beasts in their lair
Marked for the javelin, wind a belt of fire.
  Omartes scanned his walls
    And said, " Ten years Troy baffled Agamem-
      non."

Yet pile up walls, out-topping Babylon,
Manned foot by foot with sleepless sentinels,
   And to and fro will pass,
      Free as the air thro' keyholes, Love and
        Treason.

Be elsewhere told the horrors of that siege,
The desperate sally, slaughter and repulse ;
   Repelled in turn the foe,
      With Titan ladders scaling cloud-capt bul-
        warks,

Hurled back and buried under rocks heaved down
By wrathful hands from scatheless battlements,
   With words of holy charm,
      Soothing despair and leaving resignation,

Mild thro' the city moved Argiope,
Pale with a sorrow too divine for fear;
   And when, at morn and eve,
      She bowed her meek head to her father's
        blessing.

COULD DOOM NO ALTERS AT WHOSE FOOT SHE PRAYED.

Omartes felt as if the righteous gods
Could doom no altars at whose foot she prayed.
　Only, when all alone,
　　Stole from her lips a murmur like complaint,

Shaped in these words: "Wert thou, then, but a
　　　dream?
Or shall I see thee in the Happy Fields?"
　Now came with stony eye
　　The livid vanquisher of cities, Famine;

And moved to pity now, the Persian sent
Heralds with proffered peace on terms that seem
　Gentle to Asian kings,
　　And unendurable to Europe's Freemen;

" I from thy city will withdraw my hosts,
And leave thy people to their chiefs and laws,
　Taking from all thy realm
　　Naught save the river, which I make my
　　　border,

" If but, in homage to my sovereign throne,
Thou pay this petty tribute once a year ;
　　Six grains of Scythian soil,
　　　　One urn of water spared from Scythian
　　　　　　fountains."

And the Scyth answered — " Let the Mede demand
That which is mine to give, or gold or life ;
　　The water and the soil
　　　　Are, every grain and every drop, my country's :

" And no man hath a country where a King
Pays tribute to another for his crown."
　　　And at this stern reply,
　　　　The Persian doomed to fire and sword the
　　　　　　city.

Omartes stood within his palace hall,
And by his side Teleutias, the high priest.
　　" And rightly," said the King,
　　　　" Did thy prophetic mind rebuke vain-
　　　　　　glory.

" Lend me thy mantle now; I feel the wind
Pierce through the crannies of the thick-ribbed
    stone."
    " No wind lasts long," replied,
        With soothing voice, the hierarch. " Calm
        and tempest

" Follow each other in the outward world,
And joy and sorrow in the heart of man :
    Wherefore take comfort now,
        The earth and water of the Scyth are grateful,

" And as thou hast, inviolate to the Scyth,
His country saved, that country yet to thee
    Stretches out chainless arms,
        And for these walls gives plains that mock
        besiegers,

" Traversed by no invader save the storm,
Nor girt by watchfires nearer than the stars.
    Beneath these regal halls
        Know that there lies a road which leads to
        safety.

" For, not unprescient of the present ills,
When rose thy towers, the neighbors of the cloud,
  I, like the mole, beneath,
    Work'd path secure against cloud-riving
      thunder.

" Employing Æthiops skilled not in our tongue,
Held day and night in the dark pass they hewed ;
  And the work done, sent home :
    So the dumb earthworm shares alone the
      secret.

" Lo, upon one side ends the unguessed road.
There, its door panelled in yon far recess,
  Where, on great days of state,
    Oft has thy throne been set beneath the
      purple ;

" The outward issue opes beyond the camp,
'Mid funeral earth-mounds.‡ skirting widths of
      plain,
  Where graze the fleetest steeds,
    And rove the bravest riders Scythia nurtures —

" They whom thou ne'er couldst lure to walls of
          stone,
Nor rouse to war, save for their own free soil.
     These gained, defy the foe;
          Let him pursue, and space itself engulfs him."

Omartes answered — " With the towers I built
Must I, O kind adviser, stand or fall.
     Kings are not merely men —
          Epochs their lives, their actions the world's
               story.

" I sought to wean my people from the
          wild,
To center scattered valors, wasted
          thoughts,
     Into one mind, a State;
          Failing in this, my life as king
               has perished;

" And as mere man I should disdain to live.
Deemest thou now I could go back content
  A Scyth among the Scyths?
    I am no eaglet — I have borne the Ægis.

" But life, as life, suffices youth for joy.
Young plants win sunbeams, shift them as we may.
  So to the Nomad tribes
    Lead thou their Queen.— O save, ye gods, my
      daughter ! "

The king's proud head bowed o'er the hierarch's
  breast.
  " Not unto me confide that precious charge,"
  Replied the sweet-voiced seer ;
    " Thou hast a choice of flight, I none.   Thou
      choosest

" To stand or fall, as stand or fall thy towers ;
Priests may not choose ; they stand or fall by
  shrines.
  Thus stand we both, or fall,
    Thou by the throne, and I beside the altar.

" But to thy child, ev'n in this funeral hour,
Give the sole lawful guardian failing thee ;
   Let her free will elect
     From thy brave warriors him her heart most
       leans to ;

" And pass with him along the secret way,
To lengthen yet the line of Scythian Kings.
   Meanwhile, since needs must be
     We trust to others this long-guarded secret,

" Choose one to whom I may impart the clue
Of the dark labyrinth ; for a guide it needs ;
   Be he in war well tried,
     And of high mark among the
       Nomad riders ;

" Such as may say unto the antique tribes
With voice of one reared up among them-
       selves,
  ' From walls of stone I bring
    Your King's child to your tents ; let
     Scythia guard her.'

"Well do thy counsels please me," said the King.
" I will convene to such penurious feast
   As stint permits, the chiefs
     Worthiest to be the sires of warlike monarchs:

" And, following ancient custom with the Scyths,
He unto whom my daughter, with free choice,
   The wine-cup brimming gives,
     Shall take my blessing and go hence her hus-
      band.

" But since, for guide and leader of the few
That for such service are most keen and apt,
   The man in war most tried,
     And with the Nomads most esteemed, is
     Seuthes,

" Him to thy skilled instructions and full trust
Will I send straight. Meanwhile go seek my
     child,
   And, as to her all thought
     Of her own safety in mine hour of peril

" Will in itself be hateful, use the force
That dwells on sacred lips with blandest art ;
   Say that her presence here
      Palsies mine arm and dulls my brain with
        terror ;

" That mine own safety I consult in hers,
And let her hopeful think, that, tho' we part,
   The same road opes for both ;
      And if walls fail me, hers will be my refuge."

Omartes spoke, and of his stalwart chiefs
Selecting all the bravest yet unwived,
   He bade them to his board
      The following night, on matters of grave
        import ;

To Seuthes then the secret he disclosed,
And Seuthes sought the hierarch, conned the clue,
   And thrid the darksome maze
      To either issue, sepulchre and palace :

And thus instructed, treasure, town, and king
Thus in his hands for bargain with the foe,
   The treason schemed of yore,
     Foiled when the Mede rejected Scythian
     nuptials,

Yet oft revolved — as some pale hope deferred,
Seen indistinct in rearward depths of time —
   Flashed as, when looked for least,
     Thro' the rent cloud of battle flashes triumph.

And, reasoning with himself, "the Mede," he said,
" Recks not who sits upon the Scythian throne,
   So that the ruler pay
     Grains of waste soil and drops of useless
     water :

" And if I render up an easy prey
The senseless king refusing terms so mild,
   For such great service done
     And for my rank among the Scythian riders,

THE TRAITOR STOOD BEFORE ZARIADES

" The Mede would deem no man so fit as I
To fill the throne, whose heir he scorned as wife,
   And yield him dust and drops,
      Holding the realms and treasures of Omartes."

So, when the next day's sun began to slope,
The traitor stood before Zariades,
   Gaining the hostile camp
      From the mute grave-mound of his Scythian
         fathers.

Plain as his simplest soldier's was the tent
Wherein the lord of half the Orient sate,
   Alone in anxious thought,
      Intent on new device to quicken conquest.

But for the single sapphire in his helm,
And near his hand the regal silver urn,
   Filled with the sparkling lymph,
      Which, whatsoe'er the distance, pure Choaspes

Sends to the lips of Achæmenian kings,§
The Asian ruler might to Spartan eyes
   Have seemed the hardy type
      Of Europe's manhood crowned in Lacedæmon.

The traitor, sure of welcome, told his tale,
Proffered the treason and implied the terms.
   Then spoke Zariades;
      " Know that all kings regard as foe in common

" The man who is a traitor to his king.
'Tis true that I thy treason must accept.
   I owe it to my hosts
      To scorn no means, destroying their destroyer ;

" But I will place no traitor on a throne.
Yet, since thy treason saves me many lives,
   I for their sake spare thine :
      And since thy deed degrades thee from the
         freeman,

" I add to life what slaves most covet — gold :
Thy service done, seek lands where gold is king;
   And, tho' thyself a slave,
      Buy freemen vile eno' to call thee master.

" But if thy promise fail, thy word ensnare,
Thy guidance blunder, by thy side stalks death.
   Death does not scare the man
      Who, like thyself, has looked on it in battle;

" But death in battle has a warrior's grave ;
A traitor dead — the vultures and the dogs."
   Then to close guard the King
      Consigned the Scyth, who for the first time
        trembled ;

And called in haste, and armed his Sacred Band,
The Persian flower of all his Orient hosts ;
   And soon in that dark pass
      Marched war, led under rampired walls by
        treason.

Safe thro' the fatal maze the Persians reached
Stairs winding upward into palace halls.
 With stealthy hand the guide
  Pressed on the spring of the concealèd portal,

And slowly opening, peered within : the space
Stood void ; for so it had been planned, that none
 Might, when the hour arrived,
  Obstruct the spot at which escape should
   vanish:

But farther on, voices were heard confused,
And lights shone faintly thro' the chinks of doors,
 Where one less spacious hall
  Led, also void, to that of fated banquet.

Curious, and yielding to his own bold heart,
As line on line came, steel-clad, from the wall,
 Flooding funereal floors,
  The young King whispered, " Here await my
   signal."

And stole along the intervening space,
At whose far end, curtains of Lydian woof,
  Between vast columns drawn,
    Fell in thick folds, at either end disparting:

He looked within, unseen; all eyes were turned
Towards a pale front, just risen o'er the guests,
  In which the Persian knew
    His brother King; it was not pale in battle.

And thus Omartes spoke : " Captains and sons
Of the same mother, Scythia, to this feast,
 Which in such straits of want
  Needs strong excuse, not idly are ye sum-
   moned.

" Wishing the line of kings from which I spring
Yet to extend, perchance, to happier times,
 And save mine only child
  From death, or, worse than death, the Median
   bondage,

" I would this night betroth her as a bride
To him amongst you whom herself shall choose ;
 And the benignant gods
  Have, thro' the wisdom of their sacred augur,

"Shown me the means which may elude the foe.
And lead the two that in themselves unite
 The valor and the sway
  Of Scythia, where her plains defy besiegers.

" If the gods bless the escape they thus permit,
Braved first, as fitting, by a child of kings,
   Then the same means will free
      Flight for all those who give to siege its
        terror;

" Women and infants, wounded men and old,
If few by few, yet night by night, sent forth,
   Will leave no pang in death
      To those reserved to join the souls of heroes."

As, in the hush of eve, a sudden wind
Thrills thro' a grove and bows the crest of pines,
   So crept a murmured hum
      Thro' the grave banquet, and plumed heads
        bent downward:

Till hushed each whisper, and upraised each eye,
As from a door behind the royal dais
   Into the conclave came
      The priest Teleutias leading the King's
        daughter.

" Lift up thy veil, my child, Argiope,"
Omartes said. " And look around the board,
   And from yon beakers fill
      The cup I kiss as in thy hand I place it.

" And whosoever from that hand receives
The cup, shall be thy husband and my son."
   The virgin raised her veil;
      Shone on the hall the starlight of her beauty.

But to no face amid the breathless guests
Turned downcast lids from which the tears dropped
        slow:
   Passive she took the cup,
      With passive step led by the whispering augur

Where, blazing luster back upon the lamps,
Stood golden beakers under purple pall.
   " Courage," said low the priest ;
      "So may the gods, for thy sake, save thy
        father ! "

ON BENDED KNEES SUNK DOWN.

She shivered as he spoke, but, lips firm-prest
Imprisoning all the anguish at her heart,
   She filled the fatal cup,
      Raised her sad eyes. and vaguely gazed around
        her.

Sudden those eyes took light and joy and soul,
Sudden from neck to temples flushed the rose,
   And with quick, gliding steps,
      And the strange looks of one who walks in
        slumber,

She passed along the floors, and stooped above
A form, that, as she neared, with arms outstretched,
   On bended knees sunk down
      And took the wine-cup with a hand that
        trembled :

A form of youth — and nobly beautiful
As Dorian models for Ionian gods.
   " Again !" it murmured low ;
      " O dream, at last ! at last ! how I have missed
        thee !"

And she replied. " The gods are merciful,
Keeping me true to thee when I despaired."
  But now rose every guest,
    Rose every voice in anger and in terror;

For lo, the kneeler lifted over all
The front of him their best had fled before —
  " Zariades the Mede ! "
    Rang from each lip: from each sheath flashed
      the saber.

Thrice stamped the Persian's foot: to the first
      sound
Ten thousand bucklers echoed back a clang;
  The next, and the huge walls
    Shook with the war-shout of ten thousand
    voices;

The third, and as between divided cloud
Flames fierce with deathful pest an angry sun,
  The folds, flung rudely back,
    Disclosed behind one glare of serried armor.

On either side, the Persian or the Scyth,
The single lord of life and death to both,
 Stayed, by a look, vain strife;
  And passing onward amid swords uplifted,

A girl's slight form beside him his sole guard,
He paused before the footstool of the King,
 And in such tones as soothe
  The wrath of injured fathers, said submissive —

" I have been guilty to the gods and thee
Of man's most sinful sin — ingratitude;
 That which I pined for most
  Seen as a dream, my waking life rejected;

" Now on my knees that blessing I implore.
Give me thy daughter; but a son receive,
 And blend them both in one
  As the mild guardian of the Scythian River."

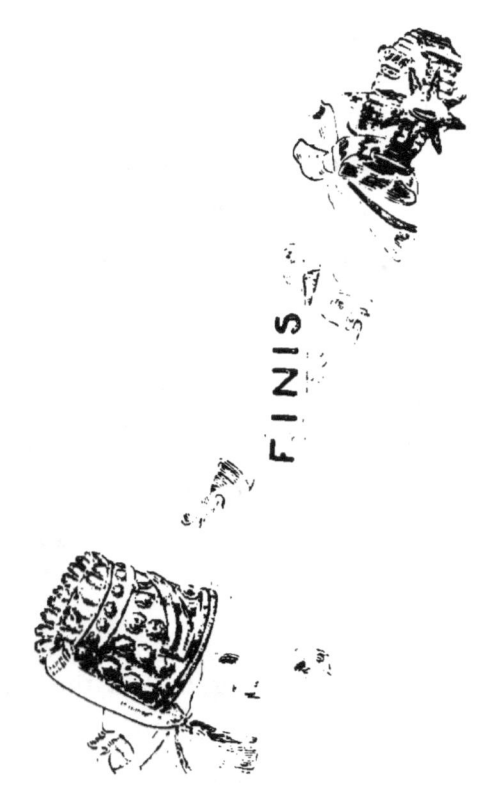

FINIS

NOTES.

* "In the market-place of the Athenians is an altar of Pity, which divinity, as she is, above all others, beneficent to human life and to the mutability of human affairs, is alone of all the Greeks reverenced by the Athenians." — Pausanias; Attics, c. xvii.

† The reader will have the kindness to remember in this and a subsequent allusion by Zariades to Greek legend, that the narrative is supposed to be borrowed from a Milesian tale-teller, who would certainly not have entertained the same scruple as a modern novelist in assigning familiarity with Hellenic myths to a Persian prince.

‡ The numerous earth-mounds or tumuli found in the steppes now peopled by the Cossacks of the Don are generally supposed to be the memorials of an extinct race akin to, if not identical with, the ancient Scythian.

§ The license of romantic fable, which has already elevated Zariades from the rank of satrap to that of a sovereign prince, here assigns to him, as an Achæmenian, a share in the sacred waters of Choaspes, which were transmitted exclusively to the head of that family, viz. the Persian King.

APPENDIX.

MILETUS — home of Thales and Cadmus, of Anaxi-
mander and of Hecataeus, the old Carian
city that the Greek sailors and merchants
raised to so great power and wealth as
to make it, five hundred years before
Christ, the greatest of Grecian cities, was at an early day the
seat of that literature and culture that made Greece the center
of ancient learning. The glory of old has long since departed ;
the ancient city on the Maeander is to-day worse than a ruin ;
even its very site is now a marsh. But the strength and beauty,
the grace and glory of its old-time culture are imperishable.
They live in epic and lyric, in song and story even to these
later days, and the reign of the scholar is endless.

Filtered through the ages, told and re-told by Pausanias and
Athenæus, by Photius and Aristides and even by that Parthenius Nicenus who taught Virgil Greek these " merry tales " of
Antonius Diogenes which were such favorites with the Syba-
rites of old live again for us in the " love-stories " dedicated
by their collecter to the Latin poet Cornelius Gallus, and in the
best eight of these caught up and put into rhythm for English
readers by that greatest of modern romancists the brilliant
English novelist Sir Edward Bulwer Lytton.

Collected by Bulwer under the general title, " The Lost
Tales of Miletus," the best of those old stories of the luxury-
living Milesians have appeared in English dress; and " The

Secret Way," the one here presented with the additional beauty
given to it by the pencil of the artist, has been selected as
the first and the best of the eight tales translated more than
twenty years ago by the English story-teller.

In his preface to his volume, first published in 1865, Bulwer
presented a long and scholarly " apology " for his work.   From
this is now taken the following extract, as showing the nature
of the " lost tales " and the character of the English translator's
work :

"Time has spared no remains, in their original form, of those famous
Tales of Miletus, which are generally considered to be the remote progen-
itors of the modern Novel. The strongest presumption in favor of their
merit rests on the evidence of the popularity they enjoyed both among
Greeks and Romans in times when the imaginative literature of either people was at its highest point of cultivation. As to the materials which they
employed for interest or amusement, we are not without means of reason-
able conjecture. Parthenius, a poet, probably of Nicæa (though his birthplace has been called in dispute), who enjoyed a considerable reputation in
the Augustan Age, and had the honor to teach Virgil Greek, has be-
queathed to us a collection of short love-stories compiled from older and
more elaborate legends. In making this collection he could scarcely fail to
have had recourse to sources so popular as the fictions of Miletus. What-
ever might have been the gifts of Parthenius as a poet, he wastes none of
them on his task of compiler. He contents himself with giving the briefest
possible outline of stories that were then in popular circulation, carefully
divesting them of any ornament of fancy or elegance of style. His work,
dedicated to the Latin poet, Gallus, seems designed to suggest, from the
themes illustrated by old tale-tellers, hints to the imitation or invention of
later poets. And, indeed, Parthenius himself states that it was for such
uses to Gallus that his book was composed.

"Out of such indications of the character and genius of the lost Milesian
Fables, and from the remnants of myth and tale once in popular favor,
which may be found, not only in such repertories of ancient legend as those

of Apollodorus and Conon, but scattered throughout the Scholiasts or in the pages of Pausanias and Athenæus, I have endeavored to weave together a few stories that may serve as feeble specimens of the various kinds of subject in which these ancestral tale-tellers may have exercised their faculties of invention. I have selected from Hellenic myths those in which the ground is not preoccupied, by the great poets of antiquity, in works yet extant; and which, therefore, may not be without the attraction of novelty to the general reader.

"I must add a few words as to the form in which these narratives are cast. Although it is clear that the Milesian Tales were for the most part told in prose, yet it appears that Aristides, the most distinguished author of those tales whose name has come down to us, told at least some of his stories in verse. The myths I have selected are essentially poetic, and almost necessarily demand that license for fancy to which the employment of rhythm allures the sanction of the reader, while it obtains his more ductile assent to the machinery and illusions of a class of fiction associated in his mind not with novelists, but poets.

"I have therefore adopted for the stories forms of poetic rhythm; and the character of the subjects treated seemed to me favorable for an experiment which I have long cherished a desire to adventure, namely, that of new combinations of blank or rhymeless meter, composed not in lines of arbitrary length and modulation (of which we have a few illustrious examples), but in the regularity and compactness of uniform stanza, constructed upon principles of rhythm very simple in themselves, but which, so far as I am aware, have not been hitherto adopted, at least for narrative purposes.

"It may be asked why in departing from the usual mechanism of our rhymeless metre, and acknowledging some obligation to classic rhythm, I did not resort to the forms of hexameter, or alternate hexameter and pantameter; for the adoption of which I might have sheltered myself behind the authority of writers so eminent, whether in the English language or the German. Certainly I do not share in the objections which some critics of no mean rank have made to the adaptation of those measures to modern languages in which it is impossible to preserve the laws of quantity that associations derived from the originals are said, I think erroneously, to demand. For certain kinds of poetry, the hexameter especially seems to me admirably suited when in the hands of a master. The time has not, perhaps, yet come to decide the dispute whether 'Evangeline' would have gained or lost in beauty had it been composed in a different measure, but most men of taste who have read the 'Herman and Dorothea' of Goethe will allow, that in any other meter the poem could scarcely have had the same patriarchal charm, and no man of taste who has read the noble translation of that poem by Dr. Whewell will venture to assert that in any other meter the spirit of the original could have been as faithfully preserved. But neither the hexameter nor the alternate hexameter and pantameter would be appropriate to my mode of treating these stories, in which, for the most part, I have sought to bring out dramatic rather than epic or elegiac elements of interest, not without aim at that lyrical brevity and compression of incident and description which is less easily attainable in the meters referred to than in composite measures of shorter compass and more varied cæsura. And for the rest, my object has been, not to attempt that which has been already done far better than I could hope to do it, but rather to suggest new combinations of sound in our native language without inviting any comparison with rhythms in the dead languages, from which hints for measures purely English have, indeed, been borrowed, but of which direct imitation has been carefully shunned."

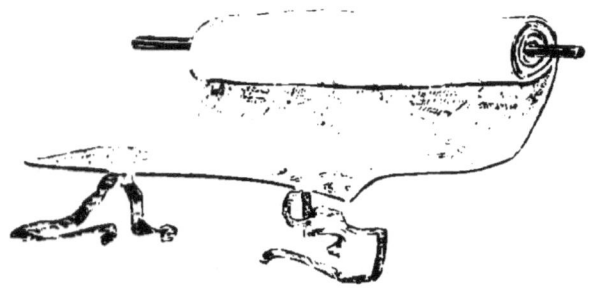

www.ingramcontent.com/pod-product-compliance
Lightning Source LLC
Chambersburg PA
CBHW030003030726
47499CB00008B/2874